The Young Scientist Book of
SPACEFLIGHT

Russian space launchings are made from the Baikonur Cosmodrome, in Asia near the Aral Sea.

Four RD-107 thrust chambers give each booster a maximum thrust of 102,000 kg.

This rocket has been the basic Russian satellite launcher from the time of Sputnik 1. This version was used to carry the manned craft Vostok into orbit.

This is the Russian spelling of Vostok.

BOCTOK

Cosmonauts' escape-hatch

CCCP

Final rocket stage which put the Vostok space-craft into orbit

Open framework connects manned section to booster.

The four boosters separate from the main rocket soon after the launch.

The boosters are fuelled with liquid oxygen and kerosene.

Central RD-108 engine gives a thrust of 96,000 kg.

CREDITS

Written by
Kenneth Gatland
Art and editorial direction
David Jefferis
Text editor
Tony Allan
Educational advisor
Frank Blackwell
Scientific advisor
Ian Ridpath

Illustrators
Sydney Cornford, Gordon Davies,
Malcolm English, Brian Lewis,
John Marshall, Michael Roffe,
David Slinn, Craig Warwick

© 1976 Usborne Publishing Ltd
First published in 1976
Revised 1982
Usborne Publishing Ltd
20 Garrick Street
London WC2.

The name Usborne and the device are
Trade Marks of Usborne Publishing Ltd.

Acknowledgements
We wish to thank the following
organizations for their assistance
and for making available materials
in their collections.
British Aircraft Corporation
British Interplanetary Society
European Space Agency
Grumman Aerospace Corporation
Hawker Siddeley Dynamics
Martin-Marietta Aerospace
Messerschmitt-Bölkow-Blohm
National Aeronautics and Space
Administration
Rockwell International

Printed in Italy

On the cover: 50 years from now,
two spacecraft take off from
Rhea, one of Saturn's moons.
On this page: Pioneer 10 flies by
Jupiter, biggest of the Sun's
planets, in 1973.

THE EXPERIMENTS

Here is a checklist of the equipment you will need for the
experiments and things to do included in this book.

General equipment

Notebook and pencil
Rule or tape-measure
Sticky tape
Glue
Scissors
Watch
Rubber bands
Paper-clips, used matchsticks
Sheet of thin card

Special experiments

Action and reaction (p. 4):
Sausage-shaped balloons
Thin wire (fuse-wire is ideal)
Nylon fishing-line or thread

Air expansion (p. 6):
Some small balloons
Narrow-necked glass bottle
Bucket and cloth

Satellite orbits (p. 11):
Ballpoint pen case
Plasticine
Fishing-line or thread

Heat insulation (p. 13):
Polystyrene ceiling tile
Two ice-cubes

Space Shuttle glider (p. 18):
Balsa wood, craft knife and
balsa cement OR stiff paper,
scissors and tape

Mars Roving Vehicle (p. 24):
Two plastic bottles (washing-
up liquid bottles are ideal)
Polystyrene foam
Stiff wire
Ballpoint pen case
Four necklace-beads

Rotating space station (p. 26):
Three plastic bottles
Thick wire
Glass or plastic necklace-beads
Two small balsawood blocks
54 cm. length of thick card
Model astronaut

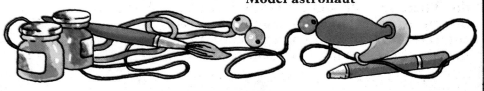

WEIGHTS AND MEASURES

All the weights and measures used in this book are metric.
This list gives some equivalents in imperial measures.

cm. = centimetres
(1 inch = 2.54 cm.)

m. = metres
(1 yard = 0.91 m.)

km. = kilometres
(1 mile = 1.6 km.)

k.p.h. = kilometres per hour
(1,000 m.p.h. = 1,609 k.p.h.)

sq. km. = square kilometres
(1 square mile = 2.59 sq. km.)

kg. = kilograms
(1 stone = 6.35 kg.)

A tonne is 1,000 kg.
(1 ton = 1.02 tonnes)

kg./sq. cm. = kilograms per
square centimetre
(1 pound per square inch =
0.07 kg./sq. cm.)

1 litre is 1.76 pints

C = degrees Centigrade

The Young Scientist Book of SPACEFLIGHT

ABOUT THIS BOOK

Spaceflight is about the exploration of mankind's new frontier. In simple language and with more than a hundred full-colour illustrations, it tells the story of the Space Age from the V-2 rocket to the present day and beyond.

It explains how rockets work and why satellites stay in orbit. You will find out about the dangers of travelling through space and what astronauts can do to overcome them. There are detailed descriptions of America's re-usable Space Shuttle, and of how an industrial base may look when men finally settle on the Moon.

Spaceflight also includes lots of projects and things to do. There are safe and easy experiments involving such principles as heat insulation and the expansion and contraction of air, and you will learn how to make working models of a revolving space station and a Mars Roving Vehicle.

CONTENTS

THE ROCKET ENGINE

No-one knows who invented the rocket. Perhaps the Chinese have the best claim. They are said to have shot 'fire-arrows' at invading Mongols in AD 1232 at the Battle of K'ai-Fung-Fu.

For the next five centuries, rockets were used chiefly as fireworks but sometimes also as weapons.

An Englishman called William Congreve made improved solid-fuel rockets around 1800, but the big step did not come until the start of the 20th century when the Russian Konstantin Tsiolkovsky suggested the use of liquid propellants.

▲Dr. Robert H. Goddard (1882–1945) did extensive research with solid and liquid fuels. In 1920 he proposed sending a rocket loaded with flash powder to the Moon, and observing the flash through a telescope when it hit the Moon.

▲It was Goddard who launched the world's first liquid-propellant rocket, in March 1926. Fuelled with liquid oxygen and gasoline, it was in the air for just 2½ seconds, covering a distance of 56 m. at an average speed of 103 k.p.h.

Action, reaction and rocket racers

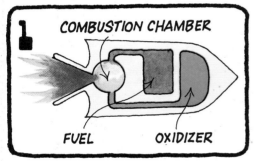

1 COMBUSTION CHAMBER

FUEL   OXIDIZER

▲A liquid fuel rocket has a fuel and an oxidizer, which are fed to the combustion chamber by gas pressure or, more often, by pumps. They ignite there. The oxidizer is needed to provide oxygen, without which nothing can burn.

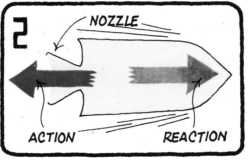

2 NOZZLE

ACTION   REACTION

▲The burning liquids produce a powerful exhaust, which expands backwards through a nozzle. The action of the exhaust causes a reaction of equal pressure pushing in the opposite direction that drives the rocket forward.

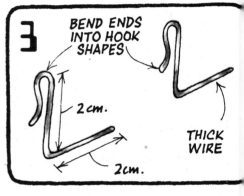

3 BEND ENDS INTO HOOK SHAPES

2 cm.

THICK WIRE

2 cm.

▲This experiment is a quick and simple way of demonstrating the principle of action and reaction. You will need a few sausage-shaped balloons, some thin wire, and a length of nylon fishing-line or thread. Bend the wire as shown.

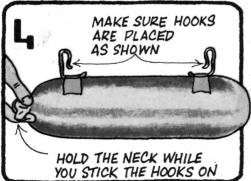

4 MAKE SURE HOOKS ARE PLACED AS SHOWN

HOLD THE NECK WHILE YOU STICK THE HOOKS ON

▲Blow up a balloon and seal the end with tape. Fix the two hooks carefully to it, making sure they are in a straight line with one another and with the balloon. Ease the tape off the neck and let the air out slowly.

5 TAPE

TAUT NYLON FISHING LINE

▲Attach one end of the fishing-line firmly to a wall or door. Stretch the line across the room, and tie or tape the other end to a chair-back or wall fitting. The line should be taut and should slope downwards a little.

6

▲Blow up the balloon again. Hold the neck firmly. Hook the balloon over the line, then let go and watch it speed forward. With several lines and a packet of balloons, you can have rocket-races with your friends.

A new unmanned rocket launcher — Europe's Ariane L3S

The Ariane is a three-stage launch rocket that is 47.6 m. long and that weighs 202 tonnes when fully fuelled. It is being built by the member-countries of the European Space Agency (ESA) listed below.

It will enable European countries to place satellites of about 750 kg. into orbit 35,880 km. above the equator. The launch base is at Kourou in French Guiana.

Belgium

Denmark

France

Italy

Netherlands

Spain

Sweden

Switzerland

United Kingdom

West Germany

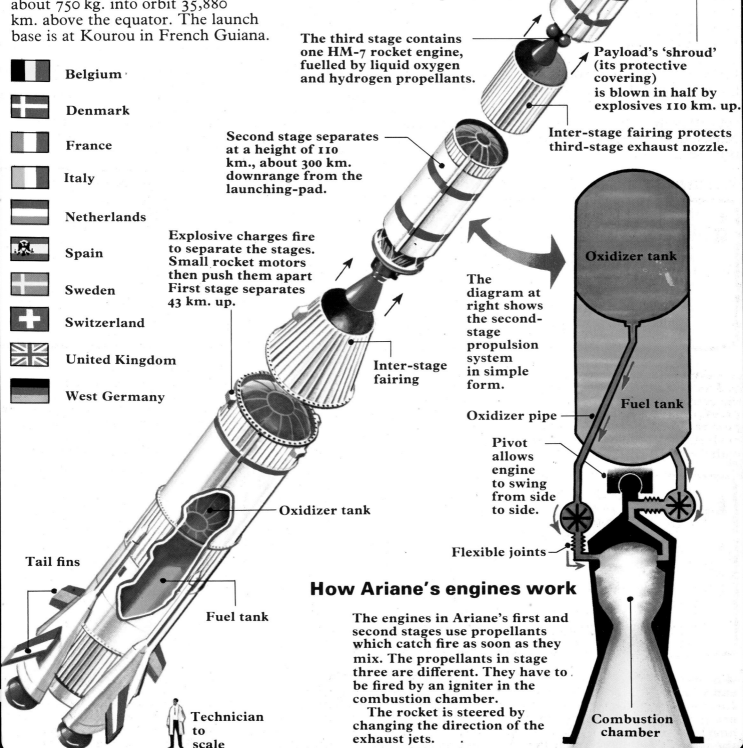

Many kinds of satellite can be carried. This one is for relaying television programmes and telephone calls.

The nose fairing—a streamlined covering— protects the payload from air friction as the rocket climbs through the atmosphere.

The third stage contains one HM-7 rocket engine, fuelled by liquid oxygen and hydrogen propellants.

Payload's 'shroud' (its protective covering) is blown in half by explosives 110 km. up.

Inter-stage fairing protects third-stage exhaust nozzle.

Second stage separates at a height of 110 km., about 300 km. downrange from the launching-pad.

Explosive charges fire to separate the stages. Small rocket motors then push them apart First stage separates 43 km. up.

Inter-stage fairing

The diagram at right shows the second-stage propulsion system in simple form.

Oxidizer tank

Fuel tank

Oxidizer pipe

Pivot allows engine to swing from side to side.

Flexible joints

Oxidizer tank

Fuel tank

Tail fins

Technician to scale

How Ariane's engines work

The engines in Ariane's first and second stages use propellants which catch fire as soon as they mix. The propellants in stage three are different. They have to be fired by an igniter in the combustion chamber.

The rocket is steered by changing the direction of the exhaust jets.

Combustion chamber

5

BALL OF LIFE

Planet Earth, our island home in space, takes $365\frac{1}{4}$ days to travel around the Sun, and rotates once every 23 hours 56 minutes. These are our years and days. Oceans cover seven-tenths of its surface, and its poles are always covered by ice.

The air we breathe is mainly nitrogen (78%) and oxygen (21%). It is warmed by the Sun during the day and cools off at night. Temperature alterations cause movements of air, as the experiments below show. The constant interchange of air between sea and land is the main cause of changes in the weather.

◀ Nine planets revolve around our Sun, the closest being Mercury and the farthest Pluto. Earth is the only one with an atmosphere that can support human life. Water, vital to us, would either boil or freeze on the other planets.

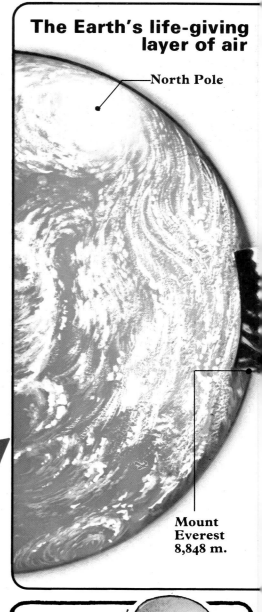

The Earth's life-giving layer of air

North Pole

Mount Everest 8,848 m.

Pluto

Neptune

Uranus

Saturn

Jupiter

Mars

Earth

Venus

Mercury

1 Expanding and contracting air

The Earth's layer of air is thin. Just 10 km. from the surface there is already too little of it for men to survive. Manned spaceflight is only possible because man has learned how to take air into space with him.

Our air is a mixture of gases, and like all gases it expands when heated and contracts when cooled.

Movements of air in the atmosphere create our weather. Nowadays satellites are used to keep watch on this (see p. 16).

2 STRETCH SMALL BALLOON OVER NECK

COLD BOTTLE

▲ This experiment with a bottle and a balloon shows how air expands when heated. Cool the bottle by running cold water over it, then stretch the balloon tightly over its neck. It will dangle loosely, empty of air.

3 HOT WATER

▲ Now fill a sink or bucket with hot water, and stand the bottle in it. As the air in the bottle heats up, it will expand upward into the balloon, blowing it up. Take the bottle out of the bucket, and the balloon will slowly go limp again.

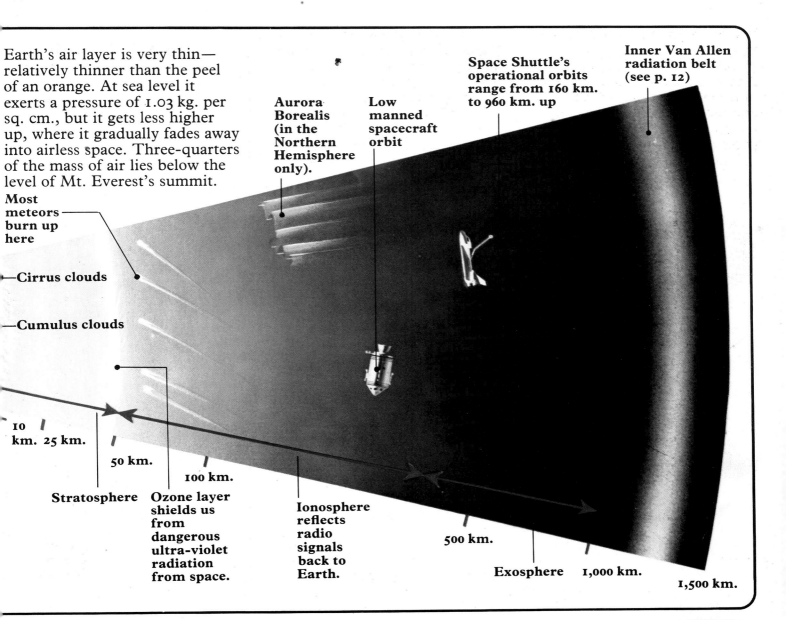

Earth's air layer is very thin—relatively thinner than the peel of an orange. At sea level it exerts a pressure of 1.03 kg. per sq. cm., but it gets less higher up, where it gradually fades away into airless space. Three-quarters of the mass of air lies below the level of Mt. Everest's summit.

Most meteors burn up here

—Cirrus clouds

—Cumulus clouds

Aurora Borealis (in the Northern Hemisphere only).

Low manned spacecraft orbit

Space Shuttle's operational orbits range from 160 km. to 960 km. up

Inner Van Allen radiation belt (see p. 12)

10 km. **25 km.**

50 km.

100 km.

Stratosphere

Ozone layer shields us from dangerous ultra-violet radiation from space.

Ionosphere reflects radio signals back to Earth.

500 km.

Exosphere **1,000 km.**

1,500 km.

4

HOT WATER

FILL TO OVER-FLOWING

▲You can reverse the experiment by first pouring hot (NOT boiling) water into the bottle. Leave it to stand for a minute while the air inside warms up, then empty it. Stretch the balloon by blowing it up a couple of times.

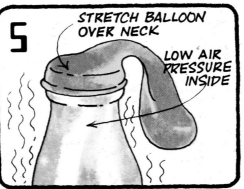

5

STRETCH BALLOON OVER NECK

LOW AIR PRESSURE INSIDE

▲Fasten the balloon over the bottle's neck. As the hot air in the bottle cools down, it will contract, causing low pressure inside the bottle. There is now higher pressure outside the bottle than inside.

6

AIR TURNS BALLOON INSIDE-OUT

POP!

▲The higher pressure outside pushes the balloon down into the bottle. In pressurized spacecraft, the higher pressure *inside* presses out against the crafts' sides towards airless space. So they need strong hulls to keep the pressure in.

DAWN OF THE SPACE AGE

The big advances that made space travel possible were made in Germany in the 1930s and '40s. After experimenting with liquid-fuel rockets with the Society for Space Travel in the late 1920s, a young enthusiast called Wernher von Braun took his ideas to the Army.

Within a few years improved rockets were being fired in secret from Griefswalder Oie, an island off Germany's Baltic coast (see map below). This then led to the creation of the big rocket research station at Peenemünde, where the V-2 weapon was developed.

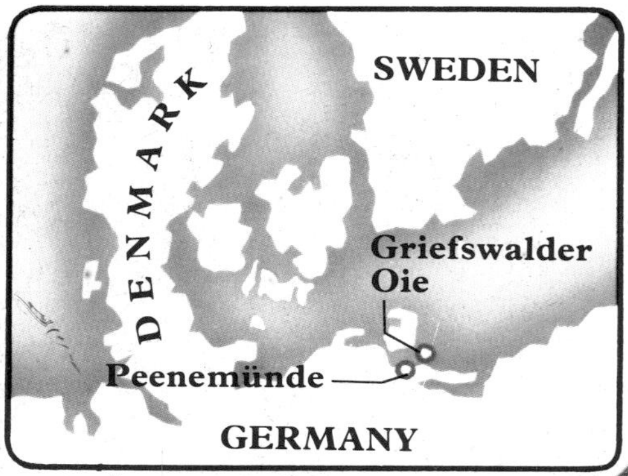

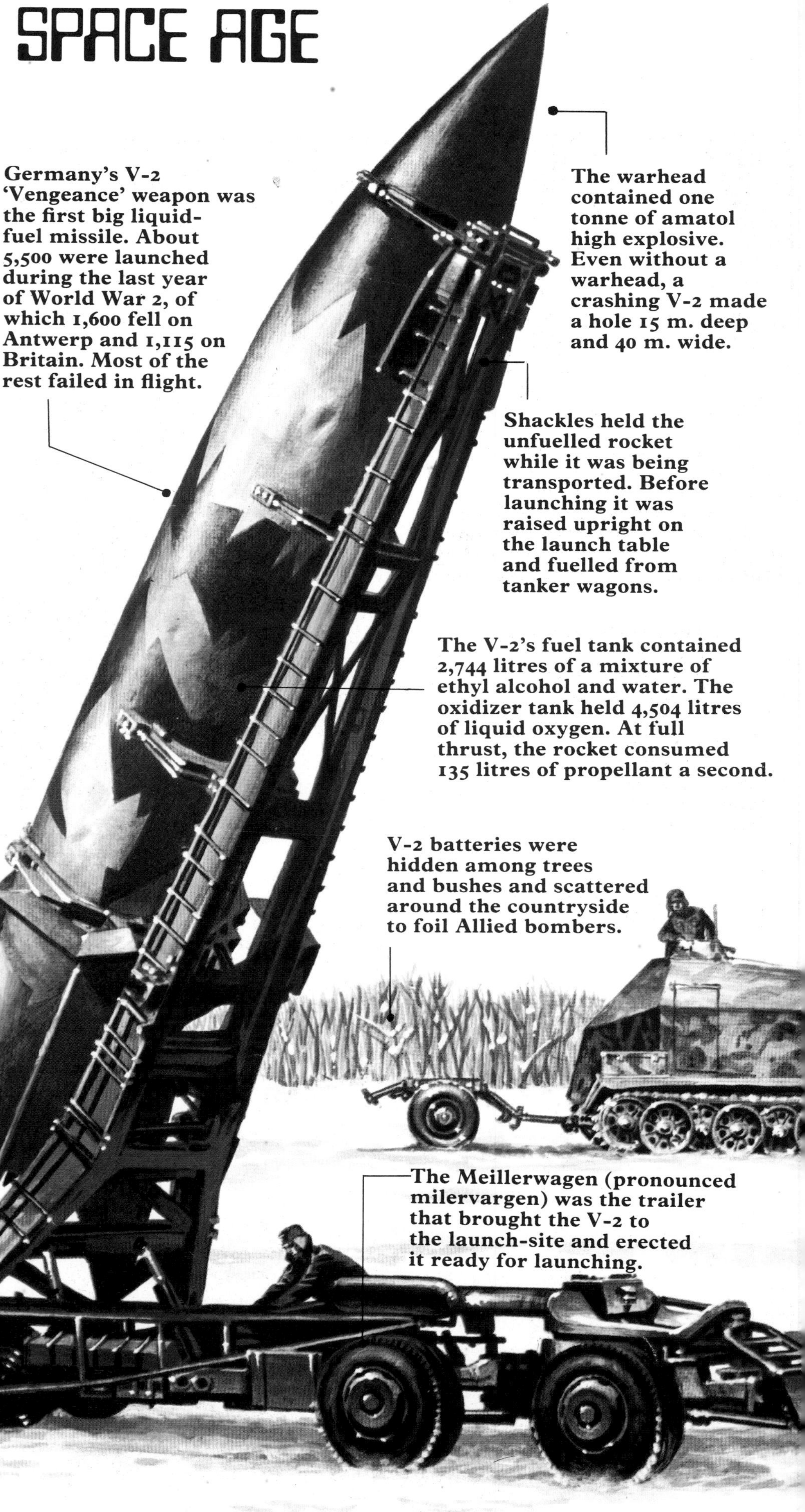

Germany's V-2 'Vengeance' weapon was the first big liquid-fuel missile. About 5,500 were launched during the last year of World War 2, of which 1,600 fell on Antwerp and 1,115 on Britain. Most of the rest failed in flight.

The warhead contained one tonne of amatol high explosive. Even without a warhead, a crashing V-2 made a hole 15 m. deep and 40 m. wide.

Shackles held the unfuelled rocket while it was being transported. Before launching it was raised upright on the launch table and fuelled from tanker wagons.

The V-2's fuel tank contained 2,744 litres of a mixture of ethyl alcohol and water. The oxidizer tank held 4,504 litres of liquid oxygen. At full thrust, the rocket consumed 135 litres of propellant a second.

V-2 batteries were hidden among trees and bushes and scattered around the countryside to foil Allied bombers.

The Meillerwagen (pronounced milervargen) was the trailer that brought the V-2 to the launch-site and erected it ready for launching.

SWEDEN

DENMARK

Griefswalder Oie

Peenemünde

GERMANY

▲A Russian schoolteacher called Konstantin Tsiolkovsky worked out that rockets would travel in airless space. Although he never fired a rocket, he drew up designs in 1903 for a spaceship powered by liquid oxygen and liquid hydrogen.

▲Wernher von Braun went to the USA after World War 2. There he led the team that launched America's first successful artificial satellite, Explorer 1. He also developed the Saturn rockets that took astronauts to the Moon.

▲A big step was taken as early as 1949, when a small WAC-Corporal rocket was launched from the nose of a V-2 high above White Sands Proving Ground, New Mexico. It reached a record height of 393 km. and a speed of 8,286 k.p.h.

A London-bound V-2 blasts off. About 500 of the missiles fell on the city.

The V-2's launching was controlled by the missile site commander from this armoured vehicle.

Launch table for V-2

Tow truck for Meillerwagen

▲ Sergei Korolev was a pioneer of Russian rocketry in the 1930s. He later developed the rockets which put Sputnik 1 and Yuri Gagarin, the world's first spaceman, into orbit.

▲ Russian scientists rocketed dogs into space in the 1950s to find out more about space travel. Laika, shown in the picture above, was sent into orbit in 1957.

A V-2 with wings

Von Braun's team also built two experimental missiles called A4bs, designed to glide for up to 750 km. The A4b was shelved in 1944, to make way for the V-2.

INTO ORBIT

On October 4, 1957, Russia shook the world by launching the first artificial satellite, Sputnik 1.

American scientists had already made plans to launch their own satellite during the International Geophysical Year (1957–58). But their first attempt failed when the Vanguard rocket toppled over on the launching-pad and burst into flames.

Von Braun's Army team was called in. Its four-stage Juno 1 rocket put Explorer 1 into orbit on February 1, 1958. The 'space race' had begun.

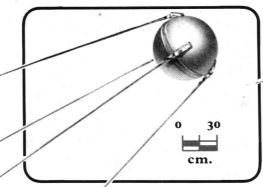

0 — 30 cm.

▲ Sputnik 1, a sphere 58 cm. in diameter, weighed 83.6 kg.—the weight of a large man. It was little more than an orbiting radio transmitter, with long 'whip' aerials. It circled the Earth for 92 days, then burned up.

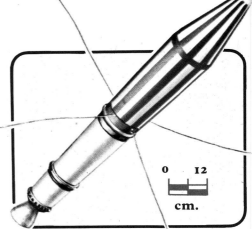

0 — 12 cm.

▲ The instruments supplied by Dr. James Van Allen of Iowa University for Explorer 1 included a geiger counter which led to the discovery of the Earth's radiation belts (see p. 12). The satellite stayed in orbit for 12 years.

Stage rockets

The manned spacecraft shown below all needed multi-stage rockets to send them into space. Each one had two or more propulsion units, which dropped off to make the craft lighter and more efficient as soon as the propellants they were fuelled with were used up.

The illustration (right) shows the launching of the three-stage Saturn 5.

The stages speed the payload up into orbit or into deep space.

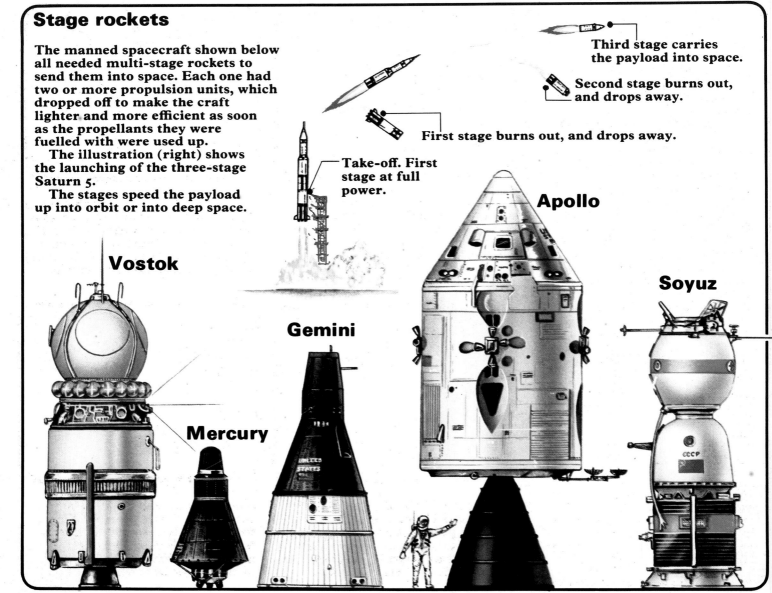

Third stage carries the payload into space.

Second stage burns out, and drops away.

First stage burns out, and drops away.

Take-off. First stage at full power.

Vostok

Mercury

Gemini

Apollo

Soyuz

▲To understand how a satellite goes into orbit, imagine a gun firing shells from the peak of a high mountain. The speed at which the shells are fired carries them a short way, then the force of gravity pulls them to the ground.

▲Suppose the gun is powerful enough to fire a shell halfway round the world. Gravity still acts on the shell, stopping it from flying off into space. It finally falls back to Earth once it begins to slow down.

▲To go into orbit, the shell would have to travel very fast indeed— at about 29,000 k.p.h. if it were 100 km. up. Gravity would still try to pull it down. But at that speed the outward pull of centrifugal force balances gravity exactly.

Centrifugal force

A satellite in orbit is exactly balanced between two forces pulling in opposite directions. One is the Earth's gravity, which pulls it downwards. The other, which pulls it outwards towards deep space, is called centrifugal force. The size of this depends on the speed at which the satellite is moving.

Because the forces are equally balanced, a change in either one will swing the satellite out of orbit—unless the other force changes too.

The pull of gravity is stronger the closer the satellite is to the Earth. This means that satellites near the Earth have to orbit faster than those farther out for their centrifugal force to balance the stronger pull of gravity.

Satellite speeds

Distance from Earth (in km.)	Orbital speed (in k.p.h.)
160	27,950
800	26,650
16,000	15,050
35,880	11,070

(At this distance and speed, a satellite seems to stand still over a fixed point on Earth. It is called synchronous orbit.)

382,000	3,620

(This is the Moon's orbit.)

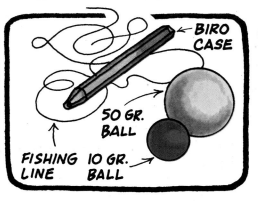

▲You can make a model satellite with some plasticine, a ballpoint pen case, some fishing-line or thread, and two paper-clips. Split the plasticine into two lumps, one five times heavier than the other.

▲The small ball will swing out, pulling the big ball up. The outward pull of the small ball is its centrifugal force. For a satellite, this must exactly balance gravity if it is to stay in orbit.

▲Thread the line through the pen case. Tie paper-clips to each end, and push one clip into each ball of plasticine. Holding the pen case upright with the small ball on top, swing the case fast in a circle.

▲Hold the case steady. As the small ball slows down, its centrifugal force lessens and it moves back towards the case—like a used-up satellite spiralling back to Earth out of orbit.

DANGERS OF SPACE

Astronauts face many risks in space, from the threat of accidents to their craft to the possibility of exposure to radiation or of colliding with meteoroids.

Huge explosions on the Sun throw out radiation that can be damaging to life. Radiation trapped in the Van Allen Belts can also be dangerous.

Spacecraft must provide enough protection to keep their crews safe in all foreseeable emergencies.

Electrically charged particles of solar wind caught in the magnetosphere gather into zones around the Earth's equator. The zones are known as the Van Allen Belts after the man who discovered them.

The magnetosphere is the area of the magnetic field of the Earth, which acts as a natural magnet, attracting atomic particles of solar wind. The magnetosphere is shaped like a tear-drop with the blunt end facing the Sun.

Earth

Meteoroid — **Bumper** — **Spacecraft hull** — **Bumper absorbs most of meteoroid's impact**

▲Spacecraft can be protected from meteoroids by a double skin or meteoroid bumper. When a particle strikes the ship, the outer shield takes the force of the blow.

Sunshade

▲Meteoroid shields also give protection against the Sun's heat. Skylab's astronauts had to put up a sunshade to keep the craft cool after its shield was torn off during the launch.

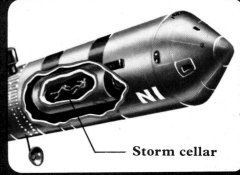

N1

Storm cellar

▲Astronauts on long voyages could avoid dangerous radiation when solar flares erupt by getting into a 'storm cellar'. Inside they would be protected by radiation-proof walls.

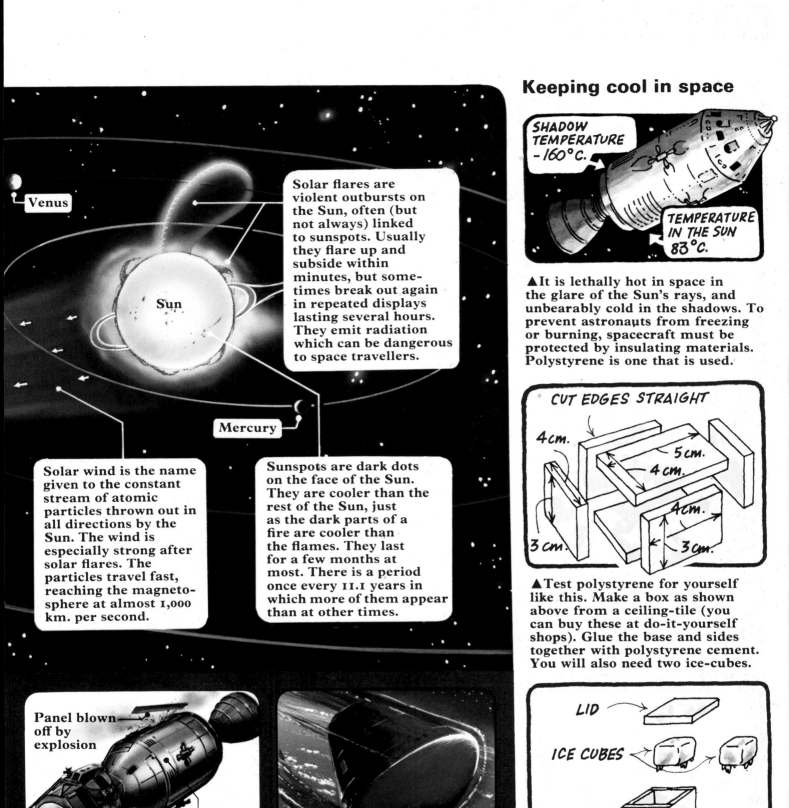

Solar flares are violent outbursts on the Sun, often (but not always) linked to sunspots. Usually they flare up and subside within minutes, but sometimes break out again in repeated displays lasting several hours. They emit radiation which can be dangerous to space travellers.

Solar wind is the name given to the constant stream of atomic particles thrown out in all directions by the Sun. The wind is especially strong after solar flares. The particles travel fast, reaching the magnetosphere at almost 1,000 km. per second.

Sunspots are dark dots on the face of the Sun. They are cooler than the rest of the Sun, just as the dark parts of a fire are cooler than the flames. They last for a few months at most. There is a period once every 11.1 years in which more of them appear than at other times.

Venus

Sun

Mercury

Keeping cool in space

SHADOW TEMPERATURE –160°C.

TEMPERATURE IN THE SUN 83°C.

▲It is lethally hot in space in the glare of the Sun's rays, and unbearably cold in the shadows. To prevent astronauts from freezing or burning, spacecraft must be protected by insulating materials. Polystyrene is one that is used.

CUT EDGES STRAIGHT

4 cm. 5 cm. 4 cm. 4 cm. 3 cm. 3 cm.

▲Test polystyrene for yourself like this. Make a box as shown above from a ceiling-tile (you can buy these at do-it-yourself shops). Glue the base and sides together with polystyrene cement. You will also need two ice-cubes.

LID

ICE CUBES

BOX

▲Put one cube in the box and put the lid on. Leave the other in the open. Now wait for them to melt. You will find that the insulated cube will melt much the more slowly, as it is shielded by the polystyrene from outside heat.

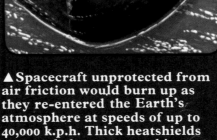

Panel blown off by explosion

Service module

▲An explosion partly crippled Apollo 13 when she was 330,000 km. from Earth. Mission control worked out a return path and sent instructions by radio. The astronauts got back safely.

▲Spacecraft unprotected from air friction would burn up as they re-entered the Earth's atmosphere at speeds of up to 40,000 k.p.h. Thick heatshields are needed to prevent this.

WHAT ASTRONAUTS WEAR

Man cannot step into airless space without the protection of a spacesuit. It wraps him in his own protective atmosphere, gives him oxygen to breathe, and keeps his body under pressure. Without these he would die.

The Apollo moonsuit (right) held oxygen in a backpack that kept the suit's pressure at 0.27 kg./sq.cm. Though it looked cumbersome, the suit was flexible enough for the wearer to walk, jump and bend. Beneath it, the astronaut wore a cooling garment in which water circulated in plastic tubes.

▲Wiley Post, who in 1933 became the first man to fly solo around the world, was also a pioneer of pressure-suit development. His experience helped his sponsors, Lockheed Aircraft, to develop an experimental pressure-cabin plane.

▲The first moonsuit was designed in 1948 by Harry Ross of the British Interplanetary Society. It had a backpack oxygen supply, flexible joints and thick-soled boots. A silvered cape was draped behind it for temperature control.

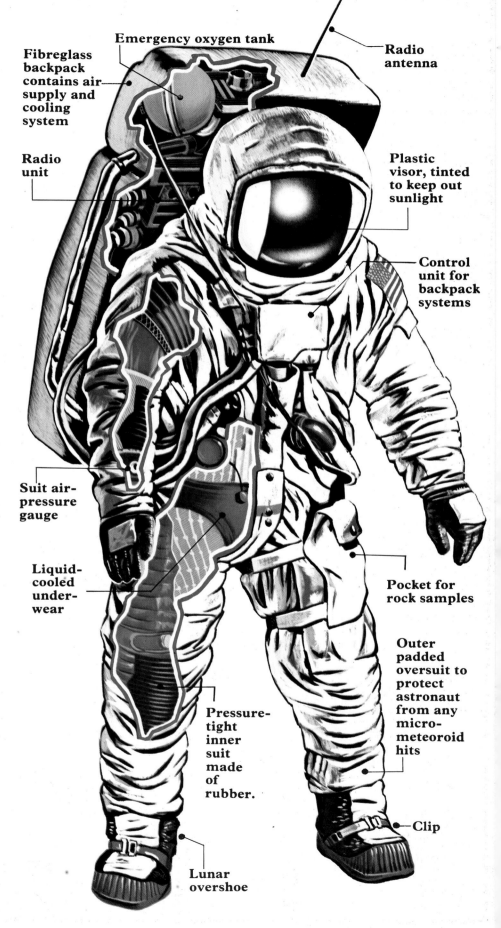

Emergency oxygen tank

Radio antenna

Fibreglass backpack contains air supply and cooling system

Radio unit

Plastic visor, tinted to keep out sunlight

Control unit for backpack systems

Suit air-pressure gauge

Liquid-cooled under-wear

Pocket for rock samples

Outer padded oversuit to protect astronaut from any micro-meteoroid hits

Pressure-tight inner suit made of rubber.

Clip

Lunar overshoe

What next — heraldry in space?

In the future, many men and women will work together in space. There will be engineers, assemblers, electricians, pilots, payload specialists and scientists. If they all wear similar spacesuits how will they tell each other apart?

On the Moon the Apollo 17 astronaut Eugene Cernan (right) wore a coloured armband for easy recognition on television screens. The astronauts also had their names on their suits.

Future astronauts may wear symbols and numbers showing who they are and what they do. Like knights of old they may work out their own brand of heraldry. Here are a few ideas. You can invent some more.

Symbols for the job . . .

Pilot

Hand holding control   Spaceship   Fireball

Communications

Electric flash   Radio mast   TV screen

Navigator

Compasses   Earth/Moon globes   Star chart

Astronomer

Sightglass   Star and planet   Telescope

Technician

Spanner   Meter gauge   Screwdriver

Moonminer

Spade   Rock drill   Explosion

. . . and how they might look on the backpack and helmet

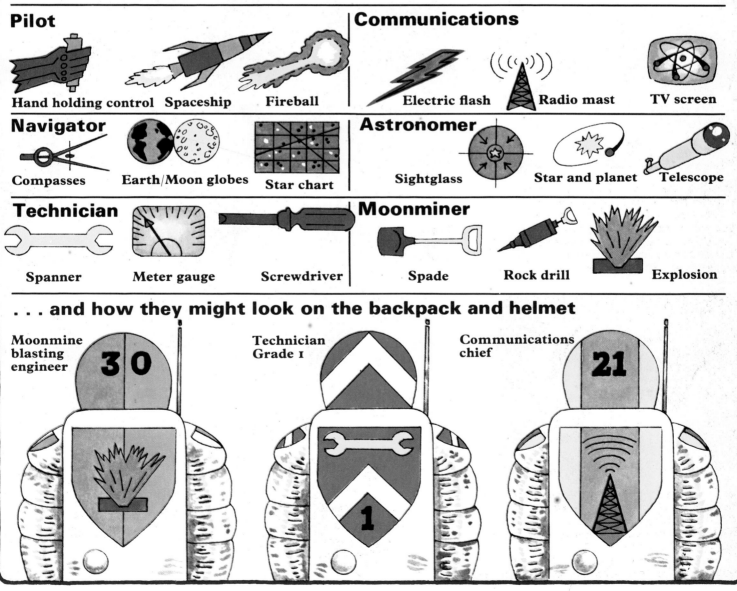

Moonmine blasting engineer   **30**

Technician Grade 1

Communications chief   **21**

SERVANTS IN THE SKY

MAROTS 2

Every day artificial satellites are helping to improve living conditions on Earth. They help us keep watch on weather changes and storms. They enable men to locate deposits of minerals, oil and natural gas.

They form a global web of communications. Because of them the number of inter-national telephone calls grew from three million in 1965 to more than 50 million in 1974. They also relay television programmes around the world.

Main body contains gas-jet controls and a combined radio receiver and transmitter called a transponder.

Reflector dish of radio antenna

LANDSAT 1

Sensory ring holds cameras and other instruments for collecting data about the Earth's surface.

Landsat's systems can map more than 161 million sq. km. a week.

Central structure contains elec-tronic equipment and gas-jet controls that keep the satellite stable in space.

'Butterfly' solar panels open out in space. They generate elec-tricity from sun-light for the satellite's power needs.

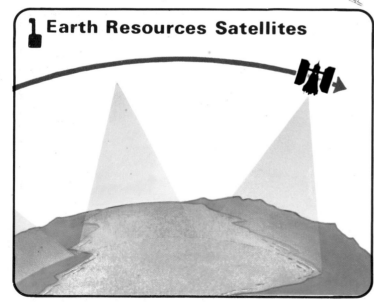

1 Earth Resources Satellites

2 Sea satellites

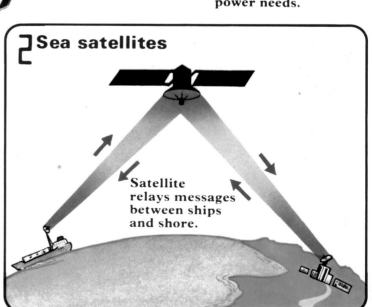

Satellite relays messages between ships and shore.

▲ Besides locating natural resources, these satellites keep track of pollution and give warning of drought, floods and forest fires. Photographs they take have many uses—for instance, they can show whether food crops are diseased or healthy. Blighted crops show up blue-black, healthy crops pink or red.

▲ MAROTS is short for Maritime Orbital Test Satellite. It is used to link ships to shore stations, and can also alert rescue services. Other sea satellites serve as 'radio stars' that allow ships to navigate accurately in all weathers, and help to control the movement of jet aircraft on long-distance flights.

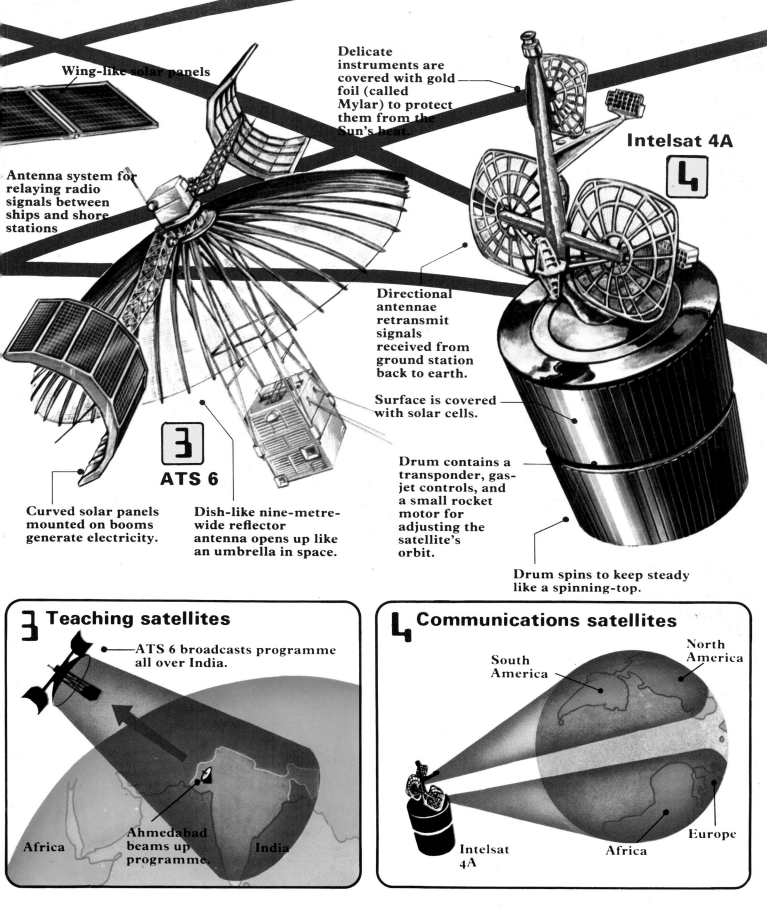

Wing-like solar panels

Delicate instruments are covered with gold foil (called Mylar) to protect them from the Sun's heat.

Intelsat 4A

4

Antenna system for relaying radio signals between ships and shore stations

Directional antennae retransmit signals received from ground station back to earth.

Surface is covered with solar cells.

3

ATS 6

Curved solar panels mounted on booms generate electricity.

Dish-like nine-metre-wide reflector antenna opens up like an umbrella in space.

Drum contains a transponder, gas-jet controls, and a small rocket motor for adjusting the satellite's orbit.

Drum spins to keep steady like a spinning-top.

3 Teaching satellites

ATS 6 broadcasts programme all over India.

Africa

Ahmedabad beams up programme.

India

4 Communications satellites

North America

South America

Europe

Africa

Intelsat 4A

▲ Satellites can be used to educate people in out-of-the-way places.

A powerful satellite stationed 35,880 km. above East Africa has been used to broadcast educational programmes beamed up from a transmitter in Ahmedabad to 5,000 towns and villages in India. Each of them had its own dish aerial and TV set.

▲ Many parts of the world are now linked by telephone, telegraph and television by satellites that keep pace with the Earth's rotation 35,880 km. above the Atlantic, Pacific and Indian Oceans. One Intelsat 4A satellite can relay 12 colour television programmes or over 6,000 telephone calls.

THE SPACE SHUTTLE 1: HOW IT WORKS

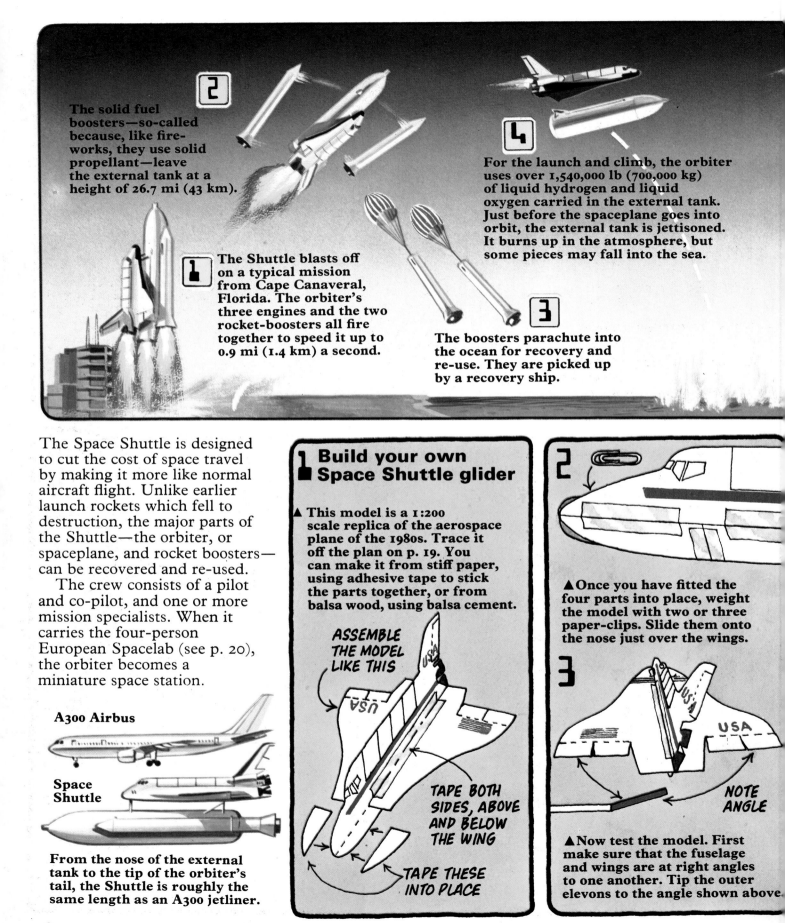

2 The solid fuel boosters—so-called because, like fire-works, they use solid propellant—leave the external tank at a height of 26.7 mi (43 km).

1 The Shuttle blasts off on a typical mission from Cape Canaveral, Florida. The orbiter's three engines and the two rocket-boosters all fire together to speed it up to 0.9 mi (1.4 km) a second.

4 For the launch and climb, the orbiter uses over 1,540,000 lb (700,000 kg) of liquid hydrogen and liquid oxygen carried in the external tank. Just before the spaceplane goes into orbit, the external tank is jettisoned. It burns up in the atmosphere, but some pieces may fall into the sea.

3 The boosters parachute into the ocean for recovery and re-use. They are picked up by a recovery ship.

The Space Shuttle is designed to cut the cost of space travel by making it more like normal aircraft flight. Unlike earlier launch rockets which fell to destruction, the major parts of the Shuttle—the orbiter, or spaceplane, and rocket boosters—can be recovered and re-used.

The crew consists of a pilot and co-pilot, and one or more mission specialists. When it carries the four-person European Spacelab (see p. 20), the orbiter becomes a miniature space station.

A300 Airbus

Space Shuttle

From the nose of the external tank to the tip of the orbiter's tail, the Shuttle is roughly the same length as an A300 jetliner.

1 ■ **Build your own Space Shuttle glider**

▲ This model is a 1:200 scale replica of the aerospace plane of the 1980s. Trace it off the plan on p. 19. You can make it from stiff paper, using adhesive tape to stick the parts together, or from balsa wood, using balsa cement.

ASSEMBLE THE MODEL LIKE THIS

TAPE BOTH SIDES, ABOVE AND BELOW THE WING

TAPE THESE INTO PLACE

2 ▲ Once you have fitted the four parts into place, weight the model with two or three paper-clips. Slide them onto the nose just over the wings.

3 NOTE ANGLE

▲ Now test the model. First make sure that the fuselage and wings are at right angles to one another. Tip the outer elevons to the angle shown above.

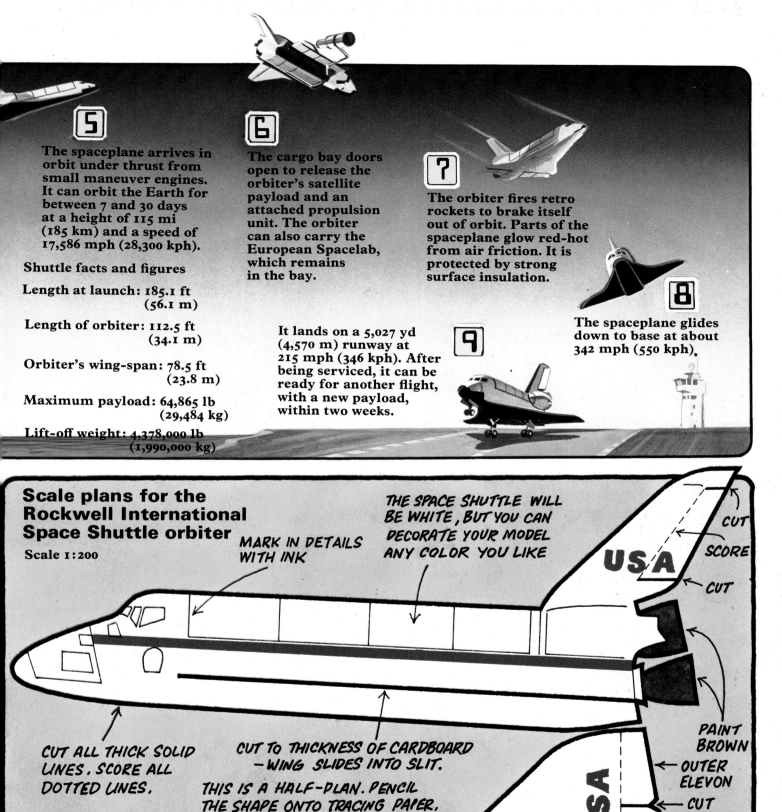

5 The spaceplane arrives in orbit under thrust from small maneuver engines. It can orbit the Earth for between 7 and 30 days at a height of 115 mi (185 km) and a speed of 17,586 mph (28,300 kph).

Shuttle facts and figures

Length at launch: 185.1 ft (56.1 m)

Length of orbiter: 112.5 ft (34.1 m)

Orbiter's wing-span: 78.5 ft (23.8 m)

Maximum payload: 64,865 lb (29,484 kg)

Lift-off weight: 4,378,000 lb (1,990,000 kg)

6 The cargo bay doors open to release the orbiter's satellite payload and an attached propulsion unit. The orbiter can also carry the European Spacelab, which remains in the bay.

It lands on a 5,027 yd (4,570 m) runway at 215 mph (346 kph). After being serviced, it can be ready for another flight, with a new payload, within two weeks.

7 The orbiter fires retro rockets to brake itself out of orbit. Parts of the spaceplane glow red-hot from air friction. It is protected by strong surface insulation.

8 The spaceplane glides down to base at about 342 mph (550 kph).

9

Scale plans for the Rockwell International Space Shuttle orbiter

Scale 1:200

MARK IN DETAILS WITH INK

THE SPACE SHUTTLE WILL BE WHITE, BUT YOU CAN DECORATE YOUR MODEL ANY COLOR YOU LIKE

USA

CUT

SCORE

CUT

PAINT BROWN

OUTER ELEVON

CUT INNER ELEVON

USA

CUT ALL THICK SOLID LINES. SCORE ALL DOTTED LINES.

CUT TO THICKNESS OF CARDBOARD — WING SLIDES INTO SLIT.

THIS IS A HALF-PLAN. PENCIL THE SHAPE ONTO TRACING PAPER, TURN THE PAPER OVER TO TRACE THE OTHER SIDE.

FRONT PART OF THE WING — CUT OUT SEPARATELY

The Space Shuttle will have many commercial, scientific and military uses. It will deliver, service and retrieve satellites of all kinds, and will be able to handle several different jobs on a single mission.

Though most of its payloads will be unmanned, its cargo bay will be big enough to carry a fully equipped manned laboratory. The world's leading scientists will be able to go into orbit in the Spacelab now being developed by ten European countries.

Unlike earlier Russian and American space stations that were abandoned in space, the Spacelab will return to Earth each time it is used.

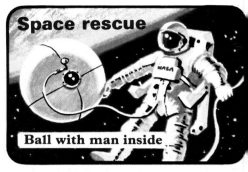

Space rescue

Ball with man inside

▲Astronauts who have to abandon a crippled orbiter could be carried to safety in NASA's 85-cm. 'Personal Rescue Enclosure'.

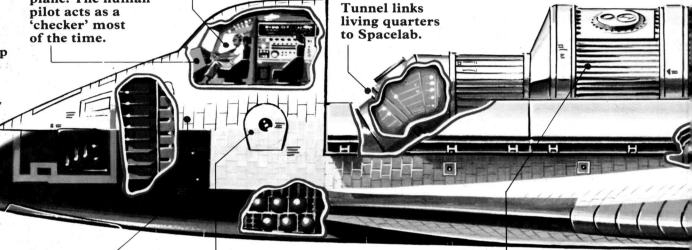

An IBM computer navigates and controls the plane. The human pilot acts as a 'checker' most of the time.

Flight-deck houses the crew—a commander, pilot, and one or more mission specialists.

Tunnel links living quarters to Spacelab.

Nose-cap protects against 1,260°C re-entry heat.

The brickwork effect is caused by heat insulation tiles fixed to the outside of the orbiter.

Hatch leads to mid-section living quarters and to flight-deck. The mid-section has four sleep bays (the crew take turns to sleep), toilet and washing spaces, and galleys with food and water.

The fully-pressurized Spacelab is 4.17 m. in diameter—big enough for four people to work in shirt-sleeve comfort. It allows scientists to work under weightless conditions in orbit.

Flight-testing your Shuttle glider

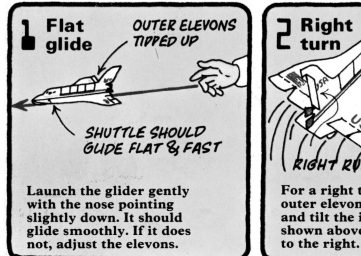

1 Flat glide

OUTER ELEVONS TIPPED UP

SHUTTLE SHOULD GLIDE FLAT & FAST

Launch the glider gently with the nose pointing slightly down. It should glide smoothly. If it does not, adjust the elevons.

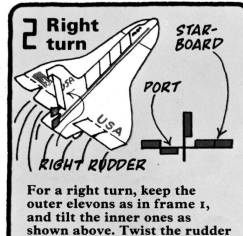

2 Right turn

STAR-BOARD

PORT

USA

RIGHT RUDDER

For a right turn, keep the outer elevons as in frame 1, and tilt the inner ones as shown above. Twist the rudder to the right.

3 Left turn

LEFT RUDDER

PORT

STAR-BOARD

USA

Simply reverse the controls for a left-hand turn. The rudder should point to the left, and the starboard inner elevon should be down.

Shuttle launch sites

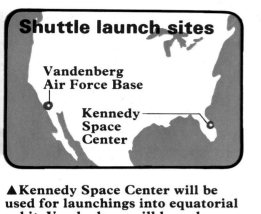

Vandenberg
Air Force Base

Kennedy
Space
Center

▲Kennedy Space Center will be
used for launchings into equatorial
orbit. Vandenberg will launch
Shuttles going into polar orbit.

Pallet
on which
scientific
instruments
are mounted.

This microwave
radar scanner,
used for studying
the ionosphere
(see p. 7),
is typical of
the scientific
payloads
the orbiter
will carry.

Two orbital manoeuvring
engines—one on each
side of the tail—
both give 2,722 kg.
maximum thrust.
They are used to
move the space-
plane into,
during, and
out of
orbit.

The wings' leading
(front) edges are designed
to stand temperatures
of up to 1,570°C
during re-entry into
Earth's atmosphere.

Main undercarriage
retracted into bay
in the wing

The three main rocket engines
each give 213,190 kg. maximum
thrust. They burn for eight
minutes after the launch, and
can be used 55 times before
being overhauled.

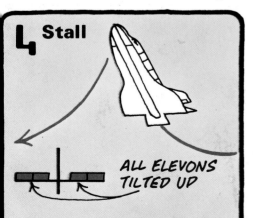

4 Stall

ALL ELEVONS
TILTED UP

Throw the glider hard with
all elevons tilted up. This
will pull the nose up, dis-
turbing the airflow over the
wings and causing a stall.

5 Gliding back to Vandenberg

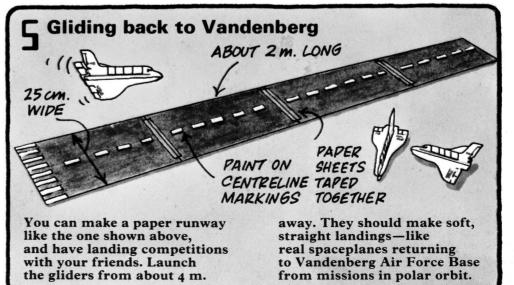

ABOUT 2 m. LONG

25 cm.
WIDE

PAINT ON
CENTRELINE
MARKINGS

PAPER
SHEETS
TAPED
TOGETHER

You can make a paper runway
like the one shown above,
and have landing competitions
with your friends. Launch
the gliders from about 4 m.

away. They should make soft,
straight landings—like
real spaceplanes returning
to Vandenberg Air Force Base
from missions in polar orbit.

INTO THE DEPTHS OF SPACE

Spacemen may not go beyond the Moon this century, but robot craft are increasing our knowledge of other planets by leaps and bounds. Not only are they cheaper to build than manned ships; they can also be abandoned if they break down.

We can fly to the Moon in three days, but reaching the planets is much more difficult. Interplanetary spacecraft must swing right round the Sun. They can only be launched when the planets themselves are in the right positions in their orbits. Journeys of this sort last for months or even years.

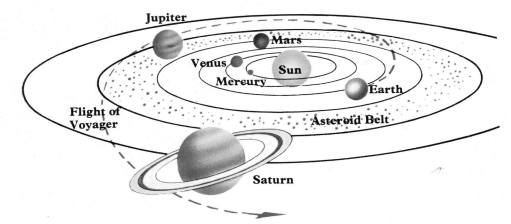

▲ All the planets shown above have been visited by space probes. America's Mariner 2 was the first craft to fly past Venus, in 1962. Mariner 9 looked at Mars from orbit, and Mariner 10 passed Mercury on its way from Venus in 1974. Voyagers 1 and 2 passed Jupiter in 1979 before flying on to the ringed planet Saturn. Voyager 2 is now on its way to Uranus, which it will reach in 1986, and Neptune in 1989. Both Voyagers will eventually leave the solar system, like Pioneers 10 and 11 before them.

▲ Mariner 10's photographs of Mercury show a Moon-like world of craters, mountains and valleys The planet has a diameter of 3,000 mi (4,828 km) and spins very slowly. Baking hot by day, it is freezing at night.

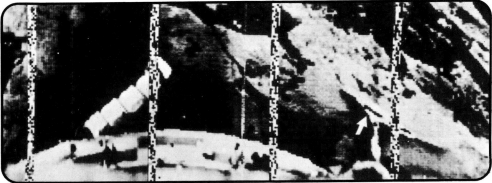

▲ Before Russia's Venera 9 and 10 swung into orbit around Venus in 1975, they sent landing capsules through its thick carbon dioxide atmosphere. Each one sent a panoramic picture by television to Earth. The first showed sharp-edged rocks, the second (above) a view showing rocks that looked like huge pancakes. The surface temperature was far above the melting point of lead, and the atmospheric pressure 90 to 100 times that of Earth.

▲ Saturn and its rings were photographed in 1980 by Voyager 1. The rings are made of swarms of ice-covered lumps of rock all orbiting the planet like tiny moons. Voyager found 1,800 kph winds among Saturn's clouds, and photographed a moon called Titan.

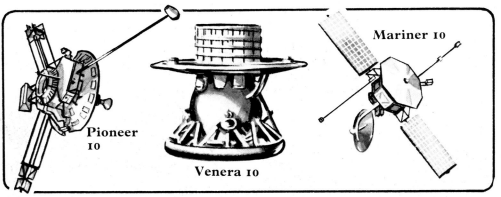

Pioneer 10

Venera 10

Mariner 10

▲ Pioneer 10 flew within 81,006 mi (130,360 km) of Jupiter in December 1973 after an 18 month journey. It confirmed that the planet has powerful radiation belts, many thousand times stronger than the Earth's Van Allen Belts. Venera 9 and 10 were identical. They sent the first pictures from the fiercely hot surface of Venus.

Mariner 10 made a grand tour of the inner Solar System in 1973–74. On its way it photographed the Earth, Moon, Venus and Mercury.

The Viking mission to Mars

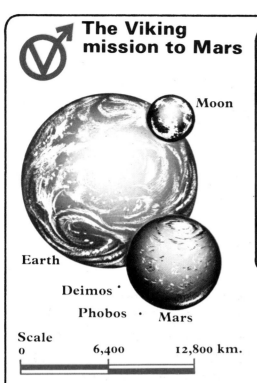

Moon

Earth

Deimos

Phobos

Mars

Scale

0   6,400   12,800 km.

◄▲The diagram (left) shows the Earth and Moon to scale with Mars and its two tiny moons, Phobos and Deimos. When Mariner 9 went into orbit around Mars in late 1971, dust storms raged on its surface. When the dust cleared, the craft's cameras revealed mountains, canyons, and features looking like dried-up river beds. Nix Olympica (above), the highest known peak in the Solar System, rears 24 km. above a flat plain. Its lava covers an area more than 1,000 km. across.

Mars 1976: Viking's landing sequence

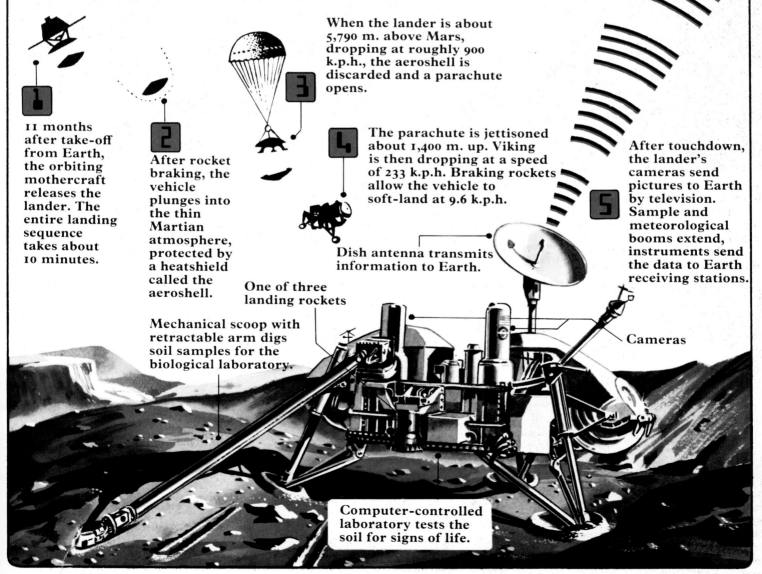

When the lander is about 5,790 m. above Mars, dropping at roughly 900 k.p.h., the aeroshell is discarded and a parachute opens.

1 11 months after take-off from Earth, the orbiting mothercraft releases the lander. The entire landing sequence takes about 10 minutes.

2 After rocket braking, the vehicle plunges into the thin Martian atmosphere, protected by a heatshield called the aeroshell.

3

4 The parachute is jettisoned about 1,400 m. up. Viking is then dropping at a speed of 233 k.p.h. Braking rockets allow the vehicle to soft-land at 9.6 k.p.h.

5 After touchdown, the lander's cameras send pictures to Earth by television. Sample and meteorological booms extend, instruments send the data to Earth receiving stations.

Dish antenna transmits information to Earth.

One of three landing rockets

Mechanical scoop with retractable arm digs soil samples for the biological laboratory.

Cameras

Computer-controlled laboratory tests the soil for signs of life.

DRIVING ON ANOTHER WORLD

When astronauts eventually land on Mars, they will want to explore farther afield than they can go on foot. They will need transport for the search for minerals and for ice or permafrost, which could be a source of water and oxygen.

The future Mars Roving Vehicle may well look like the one shown here, which is a development of the Moon Rovers already used successfully for lunar exploration. It is equipped with a pressurized cabin and a laboratory, and is electrically powered by rechargeable storage batteries.

Two Mars Excursion Modules (MEMs), each holding three astronauts and one half of the Mars Rover.

Trailer contains power cells, storage batteries, and space for rock specimens and tools.

Television camera

Pressurized cabin.

Flexible wheels are studded to improve traction. Each wheel has an electric motor in the hub, powered by batteries in the trailer.

1 Build a Mars Roving Vehicle

TOP

WASHING-UP LIQUID BOTTLE

BEAD WITH A HOLE IN IT

▲ You will need two plastic bottles, some card, a little polystyrene foam, a matchstick, a rubber band, some thick wire, an empty ballpoint pen case, and four beads with holes through them.

5

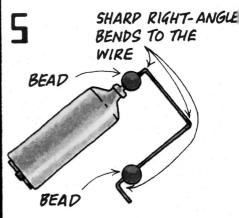

SHARP RIGHT-ANGLE BENDS TO THE WIRE

BEAD

BEAD

▲ Holding the band taut, pass the bottle-top and then a bead along the wire. Fit the top back on the neck. Bend the wire to the shape shown above, and fit a second bead onto its trailing end.

9 Testing trials

FOAM STRIPS

▲ Lift the body off again, and wind up the driving-wheel wire about 50 times. Replace the body, then test your MRV. If it skids, you can glue two foam strips around the driving-wheel.

Construction note

The sizes of plastic bottles vary, so we cannot give exact measurements. Your MRV can be any size you like, but the proportions of its parts should be as shown in frame 8 below.

2

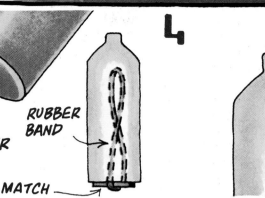

HOLE

CUT STOPPER OFF

▲ Make a hole in the exact centre of the bottom of one bottle. Ease off the bottle-top. If there is a stopper, cut it off. Select a rubber band that is about two-thirds as long as the bottle.

3

PUSH RUBBER BAND INTO BOTTOM HOLE

RUBBER BAND

MATCH

▲ Use the matchstick to push the rubber band through the hole. Once it is nearly all inside the bottle, loop its end around the matchstick. Tape the matchstick to the bottom of the bottle.

4

WIRE HOOKED ONTO RUBBER BAND

▲ With a pair of pliers, cut a piece of wire about one-and-a-half times the length of the bottle, and bend one end of it into a hook. Pass the hook through the bottle's neck and catch the band's loose end.

6 Making the body

CUT SECTION AWAY FOR DRIVE WHEEL TO REST IN

EMPTY BALLPOINT PEN CASE

▲ Make the body section from the other plastic bottle by cutting a circular section into which the first bottle can fit (see above). Cut holes for rear axle, and slide ballpoint pen case through them.

7 Rear wheels

CARD DISC

PIECE OF POLYSTYRENE FOAM

CARD DISC

EMPTY BALL-POINT PEN CASE

WIRE

▲ Make each wheel by glueing two card discs cut to the same size around a small square of poly-styrene foam. Pierce centre holes. Attach to the body with wire through the pen case, as shown.

8 The finished MRV

DRIVE WHEEL

BEAD

REAR WHEELS

▲ Fit the driving-wheel into the body, with the trailing bead midway between the two sets of wheels. Decorate the top of the MRV with a model TV camera and radio aerial cut out of card.

10

Obstacle course for MRVs

GIANT CARD DISCS SLIPPED OVER WHEELS

CARPET

OLD SHIRT

FLOOR TILES

SAND

▲ You will find that different ground surfaces will affect the performance of your MRV. The wide driving-wheel works well on smooth floors, for instance, but not on carpets. Test it over an obstacle course like the one shown above.

One way of making it go better over rough surfaces is to put giant card discs over all the wheels. Cut a hole of the same width as the bottle in the centre of two of the discs. Then slide them over the driving-wheel, one on each side of the body. Pierce a small hole in the centre of the other two, then attach them to the rear axle wire with pliers.

SPACE STATIONS

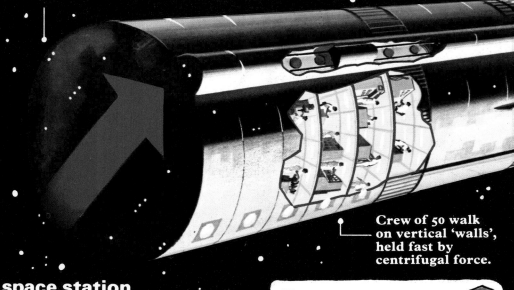

Factories in space sound like science fiction. But America's Skylab and the series of Soviet Salyut space stations have already taken electric furnaces into space.

This early 21st-century space station revolves to produce artificial gravity in the living quarters. In the control hub, which does not revolve, people are weightless.

The small diagram (right) shows how a 1980s station could be built from modules taken up by the Space Shuttle.

The station revolves 3.5 times a minute to simulate Earth gravity.

Space Shuttle orbiter carries supplies to the station from the Earth.

Lift between floors

Crew of 50 walk on vertical 'walls', held fast by centrifugal force.

Make your own rotating space station

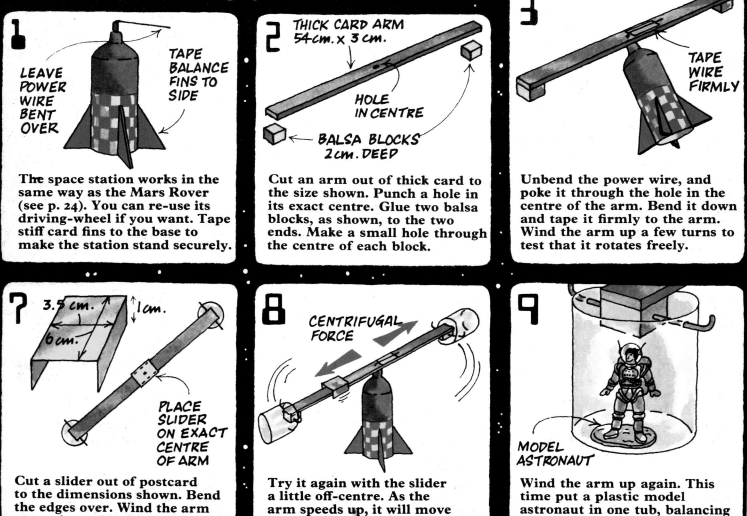

1 LEAVE POWER WIRE BENT OVER — TAPE BALANCE FINS TO SIDE

The space station works in the same way as the Mars Rover (see p. 24). You can re-use its driving-wheel if you want. Tape stiff card fins to the base to make the station stand securely.

2 THICK CARD ARM 54 cm. x 3 cm. — HOLE IN CENTRE — BALSA BLOCKS 2 cm. DEEP

Cut an arm out of thick card to the size shown. Punch a hole in its exact centre. Glue two balsa blocks, as shown, to the two ends. Make a small hole through the centre of each block.

3 TAPE WIRE FIRMLY

Unbend the power wire, and poke it through the hole in the centre of the arm. Bend it down and tape it firmly to the arm. Wind the arm up a few turns to test that it rotates freely.

7 3.5 cm. 1 cm. 6 cm. — PLACE SLIDER ON EXACT CENTRE OF ARM

Cut a slider out of postcard to the dimensions shown. Bend the edges over. Wind the arm up, and put the slider on its exact centre. Let the arm spin. The slider will stay in place.

8 CENTRIFUGAL FORCE

Try it again with the slider a little off-centre. As the arm speeds up, it will move away from the centre hole. This outward momentum is called centrifugal force.

9 MODEL ASTRONAUT

Wind the arm up again. This time put a plastic model astronaut in one tub, balancing the other tub with plasticine. Let the arm speed up gently, as in frame 6.

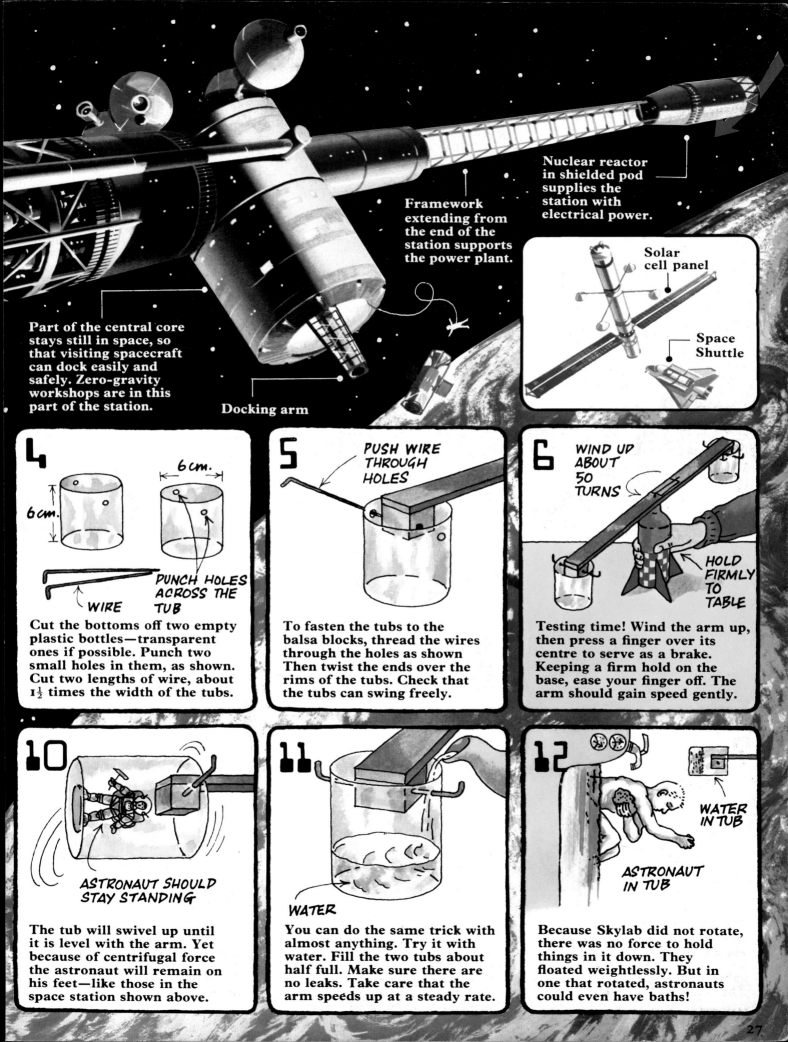

Framework extending from the end of the station supports the power plant.

Nuclear reactor in shielded pod supplies the station with electrical power.

Solar cell panel

Space Shuttle

Part of the central core stays still in space, so that visiting spacecraft can dock easily and safely. Zero-gravity workshops are in this part of the station.

Docking arm

4

6 cm.

6 cm.

WIRE

PUNCH HOLES ACROSS THE TUB

Cut the bottoms off two empty plastic bottles—transparent ones if possible. Punch two small holes in them, as shown. Cut two lengths of wire, about 1½ times the width of the tubs.

5

PUSH WIRE THROUGH HOLES

To fasten the tubs to the balsa blocks, thread the wires through the holes as shown Then twist the ends over the rims of the tubs. Check that the tubs can swing freely.

6

WIND UP ABOUT 50 TURNS

HOLD FIRMLY TO TABLE

Testing time! Wind the arm up, then press a finger over its centre to serve as a brake. Keeping a firm hold on the base, ease your finger off. The arm should gain speed gently.

10

ASTRONAUT SHOULD STAY STANDING

The tub will swivel up until it is level with the arm. Yet because of centrifugal force the astronaut will remain on his feet—like those in the space station shown above.

11

WATER

You can do the same trick with almost anything. Try it with water. Fill the two tubs about half full. Make sure there are no leaks. Take care that the arm speeds up at a steady rate.

12

WATER IN TUB

ASTRONAUT IN TUB

Because Skylab did not rotate, there was no force to hold things in it down. They floated weightlessly. But in one that rotated, astronauts could even have baths!

27

MOONBASE

When astronauts return to the Moon, it will be to set up a colony. An ideal site would be near the Leibnitz Mountains (see map below) at the south pole where the Sun never sets.

Scientists and moonminers will live and work inside pressurized shelters. There will be solar furnaces for smelting lunar ore, and solar cell 'farms' will be used to make electricity from sunlight.

This is how Man's space frontier might look in your lifetime. After the moonbase, the next step will be the planets, and perhaps the stars.

Apollo landing sites

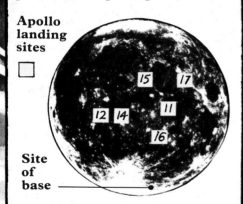

Site of base

▲Twelve men have walked on the Moon—two each at the six Apollo landing sites shown above. The last manned mission was in December 1972. No new ones are planned at present.

Astronaut using rocket backpack for quick journeys in low gravity—one-sixth of Earth's

Departing cargo pods bound for Earth orbit

The Earth

Hydroponics dome. Fresh vegetables grow here, using special liquid in place of soil.

TV camera

Container loaded with lunar minerals

Fabric-covered wire wheels

The Sun

What's what in the moonbase

1 Moondome living quarters, offices and administration centre. Domes are mostly buried underground to protect them from heat and meteoroids.

2 Radio and radar antennae.

3 Command communications centre maintains contact with Earth and supply craft. There is a three-second delay in talking to Earth because of the distances involved.

4 Lunar module shuttles between the moonbase and orbiting supply ships.

5 Solar-cell 'farm'. Panels swivel to follow the Sun.

6 Refinery used to obtain useful materials (oxygen, calcium, aluminium etc.) from moonrocks.

7 Hillside drilling leads to mining area.

8 Overhead cable conveyor carries ore from the mines to storage area.

9 Astronaut-geologists take core-samples in a survey of fresh lunar terrain.

10 Moon Rover mobile laboratory.

11 Traffic lights give warning of spacecraft approaching to land or taking off.

12 Electromagnetic catapult launches lunar materials in computer-controlled modules towards a space factory in Earth orbit. Take-off speed is more than 2,400 m. a second.

Storage area for minerals bound for Earth orbit

Landing approach radar

Landing approach lights

SPACE FIRSTS

Yuri Gagarin

1903
Konstantin Tsiolkovsky was the first man to suggest using liquid-fuel rockets.

March 16, 1926
Robert H. Goddard launched the first liquid-fuel rocket at Auburn, Massachusetts. It flew for 184 ft (56 m).

October 3, 1942
First successful launching of a V-2 rocket at Peenemünde. It flew for 118 m (190 km).

October 4, 1957
Russia launched Sputnik 1, the world's first artificial satellite.

November 3, 1957
A dog called Laika was the first living thing to go into orbit, in Sputnik 2.

February 1, 1958
The first American satellite, Explorer 1, was launched from Cape Canaveral.

April 12, 1961
Russian cosmonaut Yuri Gagarin became the first man to orbit the Earth, in Vostok 1.

May 5, 1961
Alan Shepard was the first American to enter space when he made a sub-orbital flight in Freedom 7.

February 20, 1962
John Glenn was the first US astronaut to orbit the Earth, in the spacecraft Friendship 7.

June 16, 1963
Valentina Tereshkova of the USSR became the first woman to go into orbit, in Vostok 6.

March 18, 1965
Cosmonaut Alexei Leonov made the first space walk. He spent a total of 20 minutes outside Voshkod 2.

February 3, 1966
Soviet probe Luna 9 made first soft landing on the Moon.

March 16, 1966
Neil Armstrong and David Scott aboard Gemini 8 made the first space docking, linking with an Agena target vehicle.

January 27, 1967
Virgil Grissom, Edward White and Roger Chaffee died in a fire on the Kennedy Space Centre launch pad. They were the first (and so far the only) casualties of the American space program.

April 24, 1967
Vladimir Komarov was the first Russian cosmonaut known to have died on a mission when Soyuz 1's landing parachute tangled.

July 20, 1969
The Apollo 11 astronauts Neil Armstrong and Edwin Aldrin were the first men to land on the Moon.

April 19, 1971
Russia launches the 20.4 ton (18.5 tonne) Salyut 1, the first manned space station.

May 14, 1973
Skylab, the first American space station, was launched. Skylab was the heaviest-ever spacecraft, weighing 75 tonnes.

July 17, 1975
First Russian-American space link-up, between an Apollo carrying Tom Stafford, Vance Brand and Deke Slayton, and a Soyuz with Alexei Leonov and Valeri Kubasov aboard.

July 20, 1976
US Viking 1 made the first landing on Mars to look for life, though none was found.

December 24, 1979
First launch of European rocket Ariane.

April 12, 1981
First flight of the American Space Shuttle, carrying John Young and Robert Crippen.

SPACE FACTS

One of the most amazing things about the coming of the Space Age was the speed with which it arrived. Only 27 years passed between the V-2's first flight and the landing of manned spacecraft on the Moon.

Man's knowledge of space has grown almost as fast. Here are some of the odder facts, events and theories to have come out of the years of discovery.

Because there is no wind or rain on the Moon to erase them, the footprints of the Apollo astronauts should, if left undisturbed, last for millions of years.

The most conspicuous features of the Earth as seen from space are its clouds. A visitor from space with eyesight similar to a man's would not see any sign of human life until he came within 250 km. of the surface.

At the beginning of 1980, a total of 1,019 satellites which provide (or once provided) information were in orbit around our planet. In addition, about 3,500 pieces of debris were being tracked by ground radars. This debris ranges from burned-out rocket stages to tiny metal fragments. By the start of 1980, a total of 2,308 satellites had been launched.

Because the gravitational pull of the Moon is only one-sixth of that of Earth, athletes in a pressurized lunar stadium could (in theory) jump six times higher than they could on Earth. They might even be able to strap on wings and fly like birds!

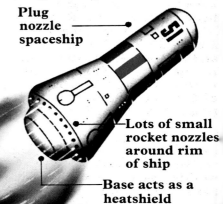

Plug nozzle spaceship

Lots of small rocket nozzles around rim of ship

Base acts as a heatshield

SPACE WORDS

A new type of re-usable space rocket has been designed in America. Called the plug nozzle spaceship, it could take off and land vertically. This wingless single-stage rocket concept has a heatshield cooled by liquid hydrogen, surrounded by a ring of small rocket engines, which are used to drive it into orbit.

When it comes back to Earth, the heatshield protects it and the rockets fire backwards to brake it down gently to land.

Pioneer 10 is expected to become the first man-made object to leave the Solar System. It is due to

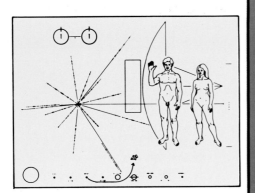

Message plaque carried aboard Pioneer 10

cross the orbit of Pluto in 1987. After that it will disappear into the depths of space. It carries a message plaque bearing drawings of a man and a woman and coded information about the Earth for the benefit of any alien beings who may discover it. It should reach the neighborhood of the giant star Aldebaran in the constellation of Taurus after 1,700,000 years.

On July 20, 1969, Houston Mission Control put through the longest-distance telephone call in history. It connected Richard Nixon, then President of the United States, with the first men on the Moon. At the time, Neil Armstrong and Edwin Aldrin were setting up a base on the Sea of Tranquility some 238,618 mi (384,000 km) from Earth.

The Apollo spacecraft which carried astronauts to and from the Moon had nearly two million working parts. A large motor car has less than 3,000.

This glossary only includes words that are not fully explained anywhere else in the book.

You will find other rocket words explained on pages 4 and 5. Satellite terms are covered on pages 16 and 17, and Space Shuttle words on pages 18 to 21.

Centrifugal force
Outward movement caused when an object moves around another. When a satellite is in orbit, its outward, centrifugal force is exactly balanced by the inward pull of gravity.

Docking
Mechanical linking of two or more craft in space.

Elevons
Control surfaces on aeroplanes or spacecraft which can operate both as elevators (to make the craft climb or dive) or as ailerons (to make it bank left or right).

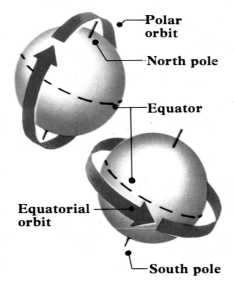

Polar orbit
North pole
Equator
Equatorial orbit
South pole

Equatorial orbit
Orbit around the equator. Polar orbit is an orbit which passes over the poles.

Fairing
Covering to protect inside parts of a rocket or satellite while it is passing through the atmosphere.

Heat insulating materials
In spaceflight terms, materials used to protect parts of spacecraft from extremes of heat and cold.

Hydroponics
Way of growing plants in water treated with nourishing chemicals instead of in soil.

Module
Section of a spacecraft.

Pallet
Platform for carrying research instruments.

Payload
The useful load launched by a rocket into space.

Permafrost
The part of a planet's surface that is frozen all the time.

Propellant
The fuel and oxidizer of a rocket.

Re-entry
The return of a spacecraft into the Earth's atmosphere.

Retro rockets
Direction of flight

Retro rockets
Rockets which fire against the direction of flight to slow down a spacecraft.

Sensory ring
Base of a satellite or space probe used for mounting cameras and other sensors—information-gathering instruments.

Soft-landing
Slow-speed landing, after braking by parachute or retro rocket.

Synchronous orbit
Orbit 237,375 mi (35,880 km) up, in which satellites match the Earth's turning, staying above a fixed point on its surface.

Thrust chamber
The combustion chamber of a rocket engine, in which fuel and oxidizer are burned.

Zero gravity
Condition of spaceflight in which astronauts and loose objects float weightlessly.

FIRST FLIGHTS

All these rockets have been drawn to the same scale, so their sizes can be compared at a glance.

You can see how the Russians made their early advances in space by launching the first Sputniks with a large military missile (2)—at a time when the Americans were limited to the tiny Vanguard (3) and Juno 1 (4).

Now compare these early launchers with the huge Saturn 5 rocket (10) which the Americans later built to send the first men to the Moon.

1 A4/V-2 (1942)
2 Sputnik (1957)
3 Vanguard (1958)
4 Juno 1 (1958)
5 Vostok (1961)*

6 Mercury-Atlas (1962)*
7 Gemini-Titan 2 (1965)*
8 Soyuz (1967)*
9 Saturn 1B (1968)*
10 Saturn 5 (1968)*
11 Ariane (1979)
12 Space Shuttle (1981)*

* First manned flight

Europe